Clifford
GOES TO
HOLLYWOOD

Story and pictures by NORMAN BRIDWELL

SCHOLASTIC INC.

New York Toronto London Auckland Sydney

To Lucinda Morgan Bailey

ISBN 0-590-44289-9

35 34 33 32 31 30   2 3 4 5 6/0

Printed in the U.S.A.

24

This is my dog, Clifford.
We do a lot of things together.

We swim together.

We play ball together.

In winter we go sliding together.

One day a man stopped us and asked
if Clifford would like to be in a movie.

Clifford had to take a screen test.
The man told him to act happy.

Clifford acted happy.

Then he asked him to act angry.

Then Clifford pretended to be in love.

The man told him to act frightened. He did.

Clifford acted sad.
The man said Clifford was a terrific actor.
He wanted him to be in a movie.

The next day they took Clifford to Hollywood.

We hated to see him go.

When the movie was finished, everybody said
Clifford was the best actor in the world.
Clifford was a star.

In Hollywood, they built him a big doghouse,
the kind a movie star should have.

They gave him fancy dishes
and brought him special things to eat.

Clifford's dog collars were made of gold and
expensive fur. Some were covered with diamonds.

He even had a swimming pool shaped like a bone.

Clifford loved being a star. They put
his footprint in the cement on Hollywood Boulevard,
just like the other stars.

Everywhere he went he was surrounded
by mobs of movie fans.

They all wanted souvenirs.

His fans were everywhere.

There were a lot of parties. Clifford got tired
of them. But they said movie stars have to go
to a lot of parties.

I saw Clifford on a television talk show.
I thought he looked a little sad.

One day he looked over his wall and saw
a girl playing with her dog. He missed me.

Clifford was tired of being a star.
That night he jumped over the wall.

He left all the fancy dishes and collars
and parties behind.

Clifford came home! And he's home to stay.
He'd rather be with me than in Hollywood.

I'm glad he loves me as much as I love him.